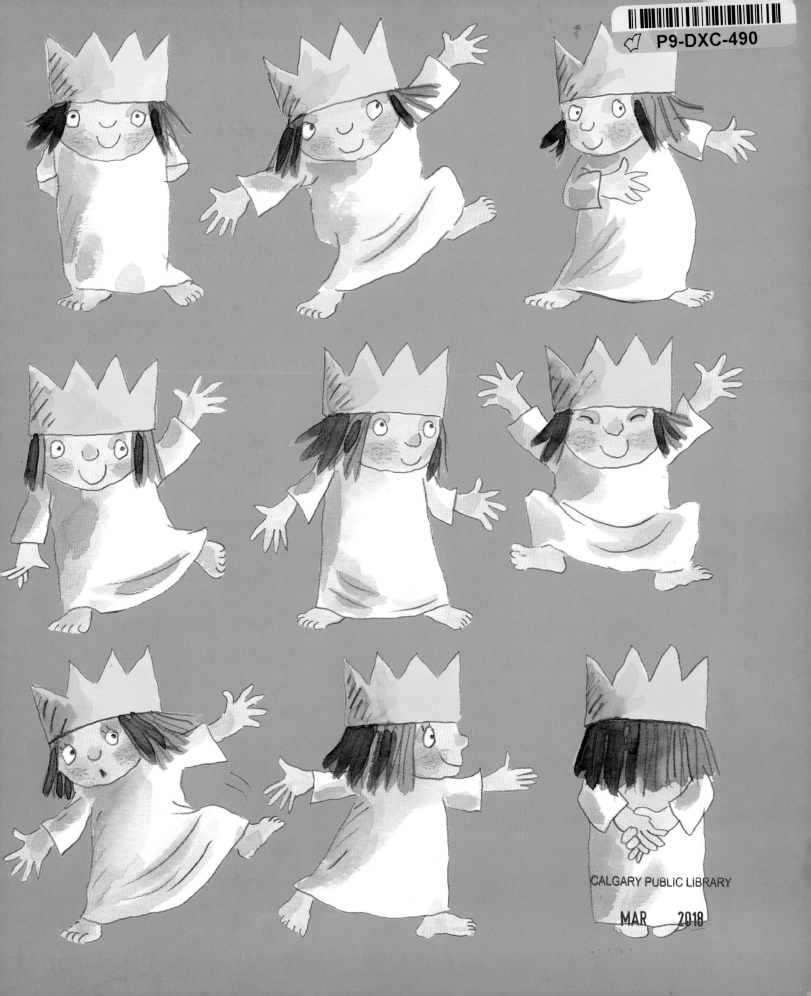

To Philippa, always innocent.

American edition published in 2016 by Andersen Press USA, an imprint of Andersen Press Ltd.
www.andersenpressusa.com

First published in Great Britain in 2012 by Andersen Press Ltd., 20 Vauxhall Bridge Road, London SW1V 2SA.

Text and illustrations copyright © Tony Ross, 2012

Distributed in the United States and Canada by
Lerner Publishing Group, Inc.
241 First Avenue North
Minneapolis, MN 55401 USA
For reading levels and more information, look up this title at www.lernerbooks.com.

Color separated in Switzerland by Photolitho AG, Zürich.
Printed and bound in Malaysia by Tien Wah Press.
Tony Ross has used pen, ink and watercolor in this book.

Library of Congress Cataloging-in-Publication Data Available.
ISBN: 978-1-5124-0598-9
eBook ISBN: 978-1-5124-0599-6
1-TWP-7/1/15

A Little Princess Story

I Didn't Do It!

Tony Ross

Andersen Press USA

"Princess!" shouted the Queen, pointing to the muddy floor.
"Look what you did!"

"I didn't do it!" said the Little Princess.
"Daddy, Mommy said I left mud on the floor, and I didn't."

"If Her Majesty said you did, then you must have," said the King.
"I didn't do it!" said the Little Princess.

"POO!" sniffed the Little Princess as she stomped
off into the kitchen.

"Did you eat all of my chocolate cake?" asked the Cook.
"NO!" said the Little Princess. "I didn't do it!"
and she ran out into the garden.

"Did you walk all over my radishes?" grumbled the Gardener.
"NO!" said the Little Princess. "I didn't do it!"
"Huh!" said the Gardener.

She found the Prime Minister looking at his tricycle
and scratching his head.
"Did you take my bell?" he asked.

"NO!" shouted the Little Princess, running toward the castle.
"I didn't do it!"

"Look at my horse," said the General. "Did you stick a bell on his ear?"
"I didn't do it!" said the Little Princess.

"Did you sink all my ships?" roared the Admiral.
"NOOOOO!" wailed the Little Princess. "I didn't do it!"

"And did you walk all over my nice clean laundry?" asked the Maid.

"I didn't do it. I DIDN'T DO IT!" sobbed the Little Princess,
and she ran away to find a friend.

"What's up?" asked the Little Prince.

"Everybody blames me for everything," sniffed the Little Princess.
She told the Little Prince all about her dreadful day.

Then the two of them climbed their Sulky Tree.

The Little Princess sat on a branch and sulked.
The Little Prince put his arm around her.

"I SAID I didn't do ANY of those things," she wailed.
"But NOBODY believes me."

"I believe you!" said the Little Prince.

The Little Princess smiled her big smile.

"Why do you believe me, when nobody else does?" she said.

"Because I did all of those things!" the Little Prince said.
"IT WAS ME...

…and I saved a bit of chocolate cake for you!"